By Arie Kaplan
Illustrated by Hollie Mengert

A GOLDEN BOOK • NEW YORK

 Published in the United States by Golden Books, an imprint of Random House Children's Books, a division of Penguin Random House LLC, 1745 Broadway, New York, NY 10019, and in Canada by Penguin Random House Canada Limited, Toronto. Golden Books, A Golden Book, A Little Golden Book, the G colophon, and the distinctive gold spine are registered trademarks of Penguin Random House LLC.
rhcbooks.com
ISBN 978-0-593-30424-2 (trade) — ISBN 978-0-593-30425-9 (ebook)
Printed in the United States of America
10 9 8 7 6 5 4 3 2 1

Loki is a sorcerer. He uses his magic to make mischief.

Loki lives in Asgard, a mythical city of heroes. He is a *prince* of Asgard, like his brother, Thor. Their father, Odin, is the king.

Loki has many powers. He can change shape, project illusions, and fire energy blasts!

When Loki and Thor were growing up, the brothers were best friends.

Together, they kept Asgard safe. Loki enjoyed playing magical pranks on their enemies. Making illusions of his brother was one of his favorite tricks!

But as the boys grew older, Loki felt that Odin paid less attention to him and more to Thor. It seemed that the people of Asgard also preferred Thor.

Loki became jealous of his brother.

When Thor went to Earth, he joined the Avengers. Thor was very popular there!

Loki stayed on Asgard. But he sometimes sneaked to Earth to play pranks on Thor.

One day on Earth, Thor visited a museum that had a medieval history exhibit. He was excited to see the exhibit's dragon statue.

“Such a magnificent creature,” Thor said, gazing at the statue. “I've fought ogres and goblins and frost giants, but never a dragon.”

Hearing that gave Loki an idea. He used his powers to bring the statue to life! Suddenly, the dragon was stomping everywhere.

Thor was ready to take it on, but the dragon was more interested in finding a way out of the museum.

ROAR!!!!

Everything was going perfectly for Loki—until the dragon wouldn't follow his directions.

"No, silly dragon. Come *this* way," he said.

UH-OH!

But the dragon wasn't listening to Loki. It began to attack him!

Loki had thought he could control the creature, but he couldn't. He wondered what he could do.

Loki realized he would have to team up with his brother to stop the dragon.

"Brother, a little help?" Loki cried. "I have a plan. . . ."

Loki told Thor his plan. Thor would distract the dragon while Loki turned the beast back to stone.

FETCH!

Thor agreed. Working together, Loki and Thor defeated the monster!

Thor was upset about all the trouble Loki had caused. But he forgave him, because that's what brothers do.

I guess Thor's all right after all, Loki thought. *If only he didn't give such tight hugs!*